WHAT REAL HUMANS ARE SAYING ABOUT THE TERRIBLES!

"A hypnotically ridiculous book! I'd love to be one of Vlad's Maggots."

—JOAQUIN, AGE 9

"I've read monster stories, but none were this original or this funny. I've read other funny, original stories, but none about a group of monsters."

—HARRISON, AGE 10

"I LOVED this book. Five out of five stars!"

—ELLIE, AGE 11

"High-appeal characters presented with plenty of laughs."

—A GROWN-UP (PRESUMABLY) AT *KIRKUS REVIEWS*

The Terribles are terror-ific!

READ ALL THE BOOKS IN THE SERIES!

Welcome to Stubtoe Elementary

A Witch's Last Resort

THE TERRIBLES

A WITCH'S LAST RESORT

TRAVIS NICHOLS

RANDOM HOUSE · NEW YORK

All rights reserved. Published in the United States
by Random House Children's Books, a division
of Penguin Random House LLC, New York.

Random House and the colophon are registered trademarks
of Penguin Random House LLC.

Visit us on the Web! rhcbooks.com

Educators and librarians, for a variety of teaching tools,
visit us at RHTeachersLibrarians.com

Library of Congress Cataloging-in-Publication Data
is available upon request.
ISBN 978-0-593-42575-6 (trade)—ISBN 978-0-593-42577-0 (ebook)

The artist used goblin blood and cursed parchment
to create the illustrations for this book.
Interior design by Jen Valero

Printed in the United States of America
10 9 8 7 6 5 4 3 2 1
First Edition

FOR KARINA ELISE AND THE REST OF THE COVEN.
BUT MOSTLY HER ON THIS ONE.

CONTENTS

RE-ELECT
CHORDIN

WHAT IS
THIS PLACE?

Well, now you've gone and done it. You found out about an island way, way out in the middle of the fish-stinking ocean where (most of) the world's monsters settled down a while back.

They're real, but they're far, far away.* Feel free to take that bit of information and repeat it to yourself a few times before bed to help you sleep better. Then, with a well-rested

---

* AGAIN, *MOSTLY.*

mind, you can focus on more important things, like organizing your sock drawer and cleaning out your closet.

However, if you have a little bit of time, you can stick around and learn some more about Creep's Cove.

That's the name of the island, by the way. Creep's Cove. Anyway, Creep's Cove was founded by a group of assorted creatures, ghosts, aliens, weirdos, and human fringe scientists* as a refuge for the monsters (and monster-adjacent people) of the world.

On this island, the residents can roam freely, work, pay their taxes, clean their gut-

---

* A FRINGE SCIENTIST (OR PSEUDOSCIENTIST, ETC.) IS SOMEONE WHO STUDIES AND PRACTICES SCIENCES THAT ARE NOT ACCEPTED BY THE MAINSTREAM. EXAMPLES INCLUDE CRYPTOZOOLOGY, UFOLOGY, ASTROLOGY, AND HAUNTED BAKING.

ters, and just be themselves. No crossbow-bearing monster hunters. No screaming, pants-peed human kids. No wretched sunlight. Yep, Creep's Cove is an honest-to-ghoulish, radioactive-ooze-dripping, volcanic-smog-drenched *paradise*.

There's even a school for kids around your age and/or maturity level. It's called Stubtoe Elementary, and it's run by an endlessly tentacled entity named Ms. Verne. You'll read about her along the way, but you're probably most interested in getting to know the kids a little better. Here's the Stubtoe Elementary yearbook. A book within a book? WOW! Have you ever loved reading something so much so fast in your entire life?

STUBTOE ELEMENTARY

ALLIE

Species:
B'lith-CHUP

Favorite subjects:
Astronomy, weird
math, dissection

BOBBY

Species:
Gelatinous glob

Favorite subjects:
Lunch, TV

EMMA

Species:
Former human-ish

Favorite subjects:
History, pickling

ERIK

Species:
Human-ish phantom

Favorite subjects:
Music, dead languages, art

OLDER-ISH CLASS

FRANKIE
Species:
Human
Favorite subjects:
Experimental biology,
meteorology, chemistry

GILLY
Species:
Swamp spawn
Favorite subject:
Ancient curses

GRIFF
Species:
(Invisible) human
Favorite subjects:
Reading, dance

LIZZIE
Species:
Kaiju, reptilian
Favorite subject:
Recess

STUBTOE ELEMENTARY

LOBO

Species:
Werewolf

Favorite subject:
(shrug)

QUADE

Species:
Sasquatch

Favorite subject:
"Oh, I think they're all really neat."

VLAD

Species:
Vampire

Favorite subjects:
Drama, hypnotism

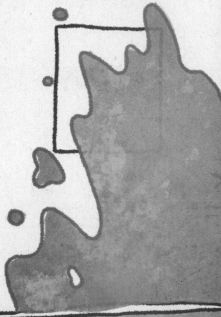

So let's dive face-first into this collection of stories. Get comfy, make sure your lighting is nice and your posture is good, take a deep breath, and imagine yourself aboard a rickety wooden boat approaching the hazy shore of (dramatic pause) Creep's Cove.

ELISE'S ARRIVAL

The air smelled like salt and ash. Elise, a long-nosed, raven-haired, greenish-skinned girl, leaned against the rail of her mom's creaking sailboat. Out on the horizon, a thick cloud of black smoke hovered over Creep's Cove.

Elise's mom ran a seasonal* resort on the island that was visited by witches and sorcerers from all over the world. Jagged Rocks

---

* AROUND THE EQUINOXES (LATE MARCH AND LATE SEPTEMBER)

Resort, Spa, and Portal to the Underworld was THE place to trade spells, work on your moontan, and relax on the beach with one of the resort's famous extra-sticky, extra-stinging jellyfish smoothies.

This was Elise's first trip to Creep's Cove. She had spent previous equinoxes with her dad, a mushroom farmer and potion designer in Belgium. Now she was finally old enough to start learning the other family business. And she'd be attending Stubtoe Elementary to get to know people of different sorts than she was used to.

"What if they don't like me?" asked Elise. "I don't *like* it when people don't like me. I don't like it at **ALL**."

"What's not to like?" replied Elise's mom. "You're my kid, and everyone likes me. I know you'll make some friends. Just be your brave self. And remember—no matter what—you're never alone."

"Right," said Elise. "I have Kimburdly." Elise pulled a bright yellow slug out of her cloak.

"No, I wasn't talking about Kimburdly."

"Ah . . . Keveen." Elise lifted her hat and grabbed a striped orange slug. "I've always got Keveen."

Elise's mom sighed. "No, not Keveen. You're never alone because—"

"Yes, I know," said Elise. "Because Mosby and Leeeee are always with me." Elise held out her arms, and two slugs, one purple and one bright white with red spots, slid out from her sleeves.

"No, Elise," her mom said. "You're never alone because your *coven** is always with you. But that reminds me. I need you to promise me that you won't turn any more kids into slugs. Give them a chance, okay?"

---

* A COVEN IS A CLOSE-KNIT GROUP OF WITCHES OR OTHERWISE CLOSE-KNIT GROUP OF ASSOCIATES.

CREEPOBALL

Elise stood at the front of a classroom full of strangers. When she'd arrived at school, she was asked to choose between a few get-to-know-you options.

1. Sing a song about yourself

2. The Hot Seat

3. None of your business

Elise chose the Hot Seat, which meant everyone would ask her one question each.

"Where do you live when you're not here?" asked Lobo.

"Belgium. In a forest."

"Are there other kids there?" asked Quade.

"Yeah. Mostly witches. Some gnomes and trolls and stuff."

"What's your favorite subject?" asked Frankie.

"Spells. And recess."

"YEAH!" yelled Lizzie.

"What's your favorite spell?" asked Vlad. "I'm a bit of a conjurer myself."

"I like turning stuff into other stuff," replied Elise.

"What's, I don't know, *cool* where you're from?" asked Griff.

Elise looked around the room. "Who asked that?"

Griff waved his pencil around in the air. "Back here. In the sunglasses."

"Oh," said Elise. "Um . . . what's cool? I guess . . . hats are cool? A bunch of kids got into making slime for a while."

Griff feverishly took notes.

"Begin.Transmission . . . ," said Allie. "What. Are.Your.Guts.Like? . . . End.Transmission."

Elise poked a finger at her stomach. "I guess they're just normal people guts."

"What is the absolute saddest thing you've ever seen?" asked Erik.

"That's a really good question," said Elise. "Seven or eight things come to mind. I'll get back to you."

"Have you chosen a best friend here yet?" asked Lizzie.

"I don't know."

"What's your favorite food?" plerfed Bobby.

"I like, um, little pies with a bunch of stuff in them."

Bobby worgled in approval.

"WHYYYYY?" groaned Emma.

"Why what?" asked Elise.

Emma's arm fell off.

Ms. Verne thwapped a tentacle on her desk. "ΛΗΒΩŒ Æμ∂℧ΘÁʃʃ⸪ ƒ℧ℑ℧oʜʃʃôℂ Øℚ∂ʃℚ⁹oℰ⩑!"

"Hooray!" shouted Lizzie. "Recess! Our favorite thing, bestie!"

"Do you have creepoball where you're from?" asked Quade.

"Never heard of it," replied Elise.

"Teams!" yelled Lizzie. "Quade, Gilly, Emma, Frankie, Erik, Allie—losers. Vlad, Lobo, Griff, Bobby, Elise, me—winners."

Griff and Gilly dropped a tarnished leather-bound trunk on the ground. Gilly opened the lid and motioned for Elise to look inside.

"Behold," said Gilly. "There be seven orbs in play, says I."

Elise scanned the trunk's velvet-lined interior. Inside were seven balls of different sizes and colors. Some were wiggling and glowing.

Vlad leaned in and pointed at each orb. "It's pretty straightforward," he said. "Wood, water, fire, stone, skin, wind, and slime. Each

19

one is connected to a specific, overlapping task worth a different amount of points."

Elise nodded along. "Okay. Makes sense."

"Great," said Vlad. He snapped his fingers. Quade lifted the velvet shelf out of the trunk, revealing an assortment of items. Vlad pulled out four shovels and passed them around.

Erik took a shovel and stuck it into the dirt. "These are the gougers. Each team gets two."

Lobo removed a massive clump of waxy, knotted twine. "This is the snarl," he said. "The team Slacker's job is to uncover the wagger. Then it's up to the Knotters to fasten three to seven of the orbs, depending on the current phase of the moon, of course."

"Of course," said Elise.

The group continued to explain how to play creepoball, interrupting each other with rules, goals, and bonuses. Elise understood

less and less as time passed. Soon she was barely paying attention. She heard little bits here and there. There were five or six different positions to play. Some players used the gougers to dig holes (maybe) to bury different orbs or carry one orb to another orb . . . or something. There were all sorts of different points to be earned: one for this, three for that, ninety-nine for something else. Then— wait—something about a staring contest?

"And that's pretty much it," said Vlad. "You can pick the rest of it up along the way."

"I'll be team Slimer," volunteered Griff. "Yeah, I'm really into slime. Slime is cool."

Lizzie moved Elise over to the snarl. "You can be our Slacker. When two orbs have been scrubbed, or when Griff glazes the slime orb, uncover the wagger. Got it?"

"I . . . maybe?"

"Great," said Lizzie. "But remember, if the water orb is within six yards of the fire orb, the Howlers are going to be all over you. And Bobby's pretty much the best Howler ever, so watch out."

"Water orb. Fire orb. Howler. Okay."

Lizzie ran to the center of the field.
"ARRRRRIGHT! LET'S PLAY SOME CREEPO—"

Ms. Verne rang the bell. Recess was over.
"AAAAWWWWWWWW!" groaned Lizzie.

As the class packed up the creepoball supplies and headed inside, Elise tapped Frankie on the shoulder.

"What's up?" asked Frankie.

"I know I'm new here," said Elise, "but creepoball seems . . ."

"Impossibly confusing?" offered Frankie.

"Yes."

"There's a good reason for that. When Creep's Cove was founded, everybody had different games and sports they played,

and as a way for everyone to get along, they—"

"Ohhh," said Elise. "They just smooshed everything together."

"Exactly," said Frankie. "Honestly, nobody understands more than half of the game. The staring-contest part makes no sense to me. And I have no idea what the stone orb is for. The key is to just focus on your

part and, well, stay out of Lizzie's way."

"Oh, but she was on my team."

"Not if the skin orb is gouged. Then we're *all* at risk."

"I see," said Elise.

"Do you?" asked Frankie.

"No," said Elise.

"Me neither," said Frankie.

TERRIBLE TOPICS:

WHAT DO YOU WANT TO BE
WHEN YOU
GROW UP?

Mayor? I don't know.

I want to run a restaurant that has games on the tables.

Ooh! I want to do that!

Restaurant-slash-games-place.

I want to be a chef.

Wow. I've never said that out loud before.

Maybe I'll run the resort when my mom retires.

Maybe I'll just wander around having adventures.

31

I want to be a songwriter for the most beloved artist in a generation:

Myself.

I WAANT TO BEEEE

BIIIGGERR.

QUADE'S GARDEN

Quade's house was tucked behind a bunch of dead trees and ashy boulders. Inside there were a few pictures of relatives on the walls and a large painted vase in the living room that Quade's parents dusted twice a day. Otherwise, it was pretty plain.

Frankie was at Quade's house one afternoon, and she noticed that he was poking at his bowl of dried fruit in what she thought might be that sad-looking type of

35

way. Then he sighed loudly, so she knew her hunch was correct. Way to be an observant friend, Frankie.

"Fun fact," said Frankie. "Sighing inflates the alveoli—the little air sacs in your lungs—providing more oxygen to your brain. The origin of conscious sighing as an *emotional response,* however, is still a bit of a mystery. So . . . is there a problem with your fruit, or do you have something on your mind?"

"The fruit's fine," said Quade. "I was just thinking about my parents. They're always talking about 'the old days' and staring at this big, dusty vase. They seem pretty sad about it."

"Really?" asked Frankie. "I had always assumed that the bigfoots . . . bigfeet . . . sasquatches here would be happy they're not being hunted and that they don't have to hide all the time anymore."

"Yeah, that part is good," said Quade. "But

they miss the forest and the sunshine. And fruits and vegetables that aren't shipped in dried or bruised and slimy. Creep's Cove is home, but it's not . . ."

"Homey," said Frankie.

"Right. I wish I could somehow give them a small piece of their old life."

"Hmm . . . aha!" Frankie had a light-bulb moment.* "Okay, then, let's give them a small piece of their old life. The first thing we're going to need is a ball of string."

"Ahhh," said Quade. "So we're going to the library?"

"Yep."

* NO SPOILERS, BUT AS YOU CONTINUE READING, THIS WILL TURN OUT TO BE A PARTICULARLY FITTING EXPRESSION FOR THIS SITUATION.

The library on Creep's Cove was run by a very particular Minotaur named Mrs. Vivlio. She had built the library as an almost-impossible maze, so visitors would tie a string to the front desk and hold on to it as they traveled through the halls. That way, they'd be able to find their way out when they were ready. To add to the confusion, Mrs. Vivlio had a special way of organizing the books. Not by title, not by author, not by subject, but by spine color. There were halls of red spines and halls of purple spines and so on. If you needed a book, you'd have to wander around and hope to accidentally find what you're looking for, or you'd have to find Mrs. Vivlio and ask. And Mrs. Vivlio was always a little annoyed that no one understood her system.

Quade and Frankie wandered through the winding halls of the library looking for either the green rows or Mrs. Vivlio. They felt like the books they were looking for were most likely to have green spines. When golden-orange spines gave way to yellows, they knew (or at least hoped) that they were on the right track.

"Look!" said Quade. "The yellows are getting yellow-green-ier this way."

"Great," said Frankie. "Let's keep going.

And as soon as things get green-green, start looking at titles."

At a fork in the maze, they chose a direction that felt more *forest* green than *lime* green. That's when they almost bumped directly into Mrs. Vivlio.

"Are we finding everything we need, children?" she asked.

"Not yet," said Frankie. "We're looking for some books on greenhouses and gardening."

"Then why are you in *this* section of the

library?" Mrs. Vivlio shook her head in judgy disappointment. "Follow me."

She took off down the aisle, and Frankie and Quade ran after her. They struggled to unwind the string as they went along. They considered dropping it so they could keep up, but getting lost in the library was too scary to risk.

They turned, they doubled back, they

climbed up and down stairs, they jumped over holes in the floor. The books on the shelves went from green to brown to orange to black to pink to blue. Here and there, Mrs. Vivlio grabbed books and handed them to the kids. *Greenhouses of Absolute Trash* by Pip Bauble. *Small-Scale Farming for Goblins* by Yobble Throte. *Rotten Gold: Composting Is So Gross!* by Cramilla Chipsington, foreword by Daisy Portu. *Dirt, Water, Seeds, and Patience If You Can Even Stand It* by Jaye Salem.

"Good?" asked Mrs. Vivlio.

"Great!" answered Quade and Frankie.

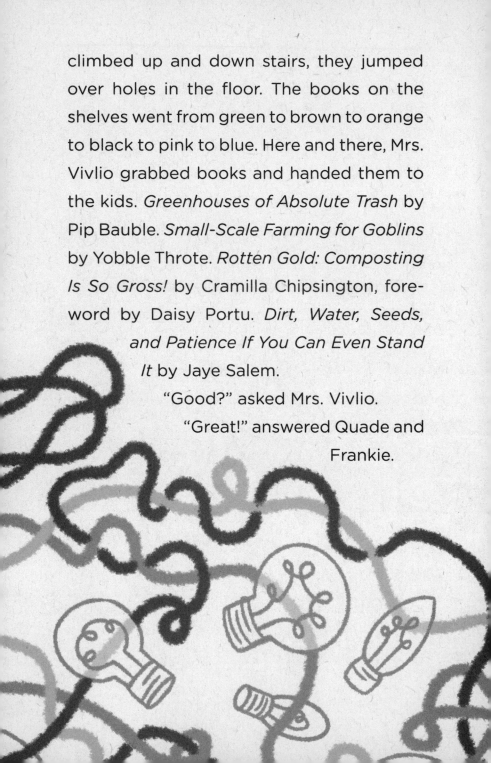

"Hellllp!" cried a voice in the distance.

Mrs. Vivlio sighed, turned, and jumped down a hole.

Quade and Frankie followed the string back the way they'd come. When they finally reached the front desk, a reverse mermaid scanned their library cards and checked out their books. "Two weeks on all of these," she said. "After that it's one toe per day."

Back in Frankie's lab, Frankie and Quade pored over their library books, sketched ideas, and made a list of materials they'd need for a greenhouse mini-forest wonderland. They decided on a barn-shaped design that was about thirteen feet by twenty feet. Then they gathered wires and some giant light bulbs.

There was always plenty of that sort of thing at Frankie's house.

Their next stop was the harbor. The dockworkers maintained a huge scrap area of unclaimed and damaged junk that had been shipped in, so Frankie figured she and Quade could get a lot of what they needed there. When they got to the gate, they were greeted by a stitched-up patchwork of a boy wearing a beanie.

"Hey, Mom!" shouted Adam. "I mean— Hi, Frankie! Heya, Quade."

"Heya, Adam," said Quade.

A few months earlier, Frankie had built Adam from spare parts in her lab, and he still sometimes called her Mom out of habit. Adam was enrolled in the little-kid class at school, and he had a job at the docks after school and on weekends.

Frankie handed Adam her list. "We're looking for some stuff to build a greenhouse."

Adam scanned the list. "Yeeeeeah, I think we got a lotta this stuff in the scrap heap. I'll give ya a hand."

The scrap heap really delivered. Adam helped Frankie and Quade load lumber, old windows, shelves, a half-dozen cracked flowerpots, and some plastic and metal sheets in the back of his truck. "No charge,

by the way. Yous're doin' me a favor unloading this stuff."

On the way to Quade's backyard, they stopped at the hardware store for nails, duct tape, and a few large trash cans.

Then it was a matter of putting it all together. They used the lumber to build a frame. They added sheeting for the walls and the ceiling, and then windows so air could flow through. Inside the structure, they set up some shelves and arranged the pots and containers they had gathered. Then they wired up the bulbs and hung them overhead.

The easiest part was the soil. Creep's Cove might have been one of the gloomi-

5

est, smelliest, darkest places on earth, but the volcanic soil was rich in nutrients, and there was more than enough to fill every pot and container in the greenhouse. Soon the greenhouse would be full of healthy—

"**PLANTS!**" yelled Frankie. "We forgot all about plants!"

"Oh, yeah," said Quade.

Frankie and Quade ran all over the neighborhood looking for seeds to plant. Bobby had some old trail mix in the back of his pantry, but it turned out to be just chocolate bits, gummy worms, and regular worms. The owner of Heck's Cauldron, a talisman-and-curses shop, tried to sell them

some magic beans, but nobody falls for that anymore. Frankie's dad offered some of the plants he had in his lab, but they were the rudest, loudest plants ever zapped into existence.

"Any other ideas?" asked Frankie.

"I guess we can see what we dig out of the half-rotten veggies at my house."

Back at the greenhouse, Quade was feeling disappointed. He and Frankie had worked really hard to build something nice for his parents, but ultimately it was just a box of dirt. He was rotating a pot to face its crack against the wall when he heard a voice behind him.

"What in the world is all this?"

Quade turned and saw his parents standing in the doorway to the greenhouse. They were looking around the room with their mouths and eyes wide open.

"It's . . . I wanted it to be something," said Quade, "but it's basically nothing."

Quade's mom sprinted toward the house and threw the back door open so hard that it slammed against the wall.

"I'm sorry. We'll take it down. We were trying to—"

Quade's mom burst through the back door and into the greenhouse. She was holding the painted vase from the living room. Quade's dad smiled and took off the lid. "Take a look, Q," he said.

Quade reached in and pulled out a dozen tiny envelopes. Each one had small words written on the front. "'Alpine strawberry,'" read Quade. "'Cape gooseberry.' 'Rat's tail radish.' 'Honeysuckle.' These are all *seeds*. From back home?"

"*This* is home," said Quade's mom. "Because of you. Thank you for this. And thank you, Frankie."

Quade, his parents, and Frankie spent an hour planting seeds in the greenhouse. While they were watering them, Quade looked around and shrugged. "I guess it's still just a glass box of dirt for a while. It could be weeks before it starts looking foresty in here."

Frankie squinted in a schemy way. "Not if *science* has anything to say about that," she said. "I haven't found a problem that can't be solved by a laser and/or a lot of colorful liquids mixed together. And if that doesn't work, we're friends with a witch."

FOOD ETERNAL

Hey! Don't toss those scraps! Start your own tiny farm with a few items and a little patience.

You'll need:
a shallow dish or bowl
a small planter or pot
potting soil
kitchen scraps *

(bowl, takeout container, etc.)

POTTING SOIL

* works with: (easiest)
bok choy, green onion, onion, cabbage, celery, lettuce, leek, garlic, shallot, lemongrass, etc.

try a clove of garlic

edible greens or a whole bulb in, gosh, 9 months?

*Sorta works with: carrot, radish, beet, turnip (you won't get new edible roots, but the greens are suuuper tasty)

(GROWING FOOD FROM KITCHEN SCRAPS)

①

Place the bottom 1" of your veggie scraps in a shallow dish of water, rooty side down.

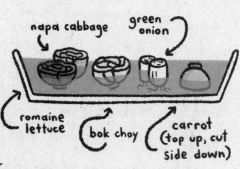

napa cabbage

green onion

romaine lettuce

bok choy

carrot (top up, cut side down)

②

Put in a sunny spot or under a grow light and change the water every day or so.

new growth!

③

When a nice set of roots and some new growth appears, plant the lil' guys in a pot of soil in a sunny spot.

(3-7 days)

cut and eat and cut and eat...

THE WITCHY RESORT

Elise passed out little cards to each member of Ms. Verne's older-ish class. The cards had instructions to gather by the playground after school for a special announcement.

"The haunted playground or the sticky playground?" thubbed Bobby.

"Oh—which one has the broken slide?" asked Elise.

"The sticky playground," replied Quade.

"Then I meant the sticky playground," said Elise.

"The sticky playground is closed," said Erik. "It got too sticky."

"Well, we aren't going to *use* the playground," said Elise. "We're just meeting by it."

"But I might want to seesaw later," grumbled Lizzie. "Why are you trying to stop me from seesawing? What in the world is your personal problem with me seesawing, bestie?"

"Fine," said Elise. "Let's all meet by the haunted playground."

"WHAT DO YOU CHILDREN WANT?!" demanded a melty-faced spirit from the swing set.

"We're just having a meeting," said Elise. "Go about your business, ghost."

"Wooooooo-ooooooooooooo," moaned the ghost.

Elise pulled a small book from her cloak, opened it to a page marked by a purple ribbon, read a passage to herself, and nodded. **"CAULDRONICUS APPAPERIUM!"** she yelled. A black cauldron appeared next to her in a puff of green smoke.

"New friends, I am pleased to announce that my mother has allowed me to invite two guests to a day at Jagged Rocks Resort, Spa, and Portal to the Underworld."

"Ooh!" exclaimed Lizzie. "Who are you bringing, bestie? Who else, I mean."

"Who indeed," replied Elise. "In order to be fair, I will be selecting names at random. Please drop the cards I passed out this morning into the cauldron."

"I accidentally absorbed mine on the way over," glurfed Bobby.

"I left mine in my desk," said Lobo.

"Begin.Transmission . . . Oops.This.Being. Recycled.The.Item.After.Reading.As.This. Being.Believed.The.Item.Was.No.Longer. Needed . . . End.Transmission," said Allie.

Elise snapped her fingers, and three new cards appeared, hovering over the cauldron. They dropped inside. "There," said Elise.

The rest of the kids tossed their names into the cauldron.

"What spell are you going to use to select the names?" asked Griff.

"Oh," said Elise. "I was just going to reach in and grab two cards."

"Feels a bit anticlimactic," said Erik.

"I'll make a big show of it," offered Elise. "How about that?"

Erik nodded.

"Behold!" announced Elise, reaching into the cauldron. "The first guest shall be . . ." Elise dramatically pulled a name from the cauldron. "Gilly!"

"Verily!" shouted Gilly.

The rest of the group clapped.

"And now . . . the second and final guest at Jagged

Rocks Resort, Spa, and Portal to the Underworld shall be . . ." Elise flailed her arm, dipped into the cauldron, and waaaaaved the selected card up to her face. She cleared her throat and read the name at the top of the card. "Vlad!"

"YESSS!" hissed Vlad. He was already thinking about his resort-wear look. *Linen shirt and patterned shorts? Blazer or no blazer? Flip-flops or slippers? Captain's hat? DARE I?* The rest of the class, except for Lizzie, clapped.

Elise clapped her hands, then pointed at the cauldron. **"MUIREPAPPA SUCINORDLUAC!"** The cauldron vanished in a puff of smoke.

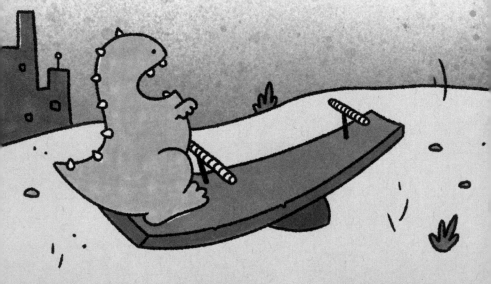

"And now I wish you all good day. Gilly, Vlad—meet me at the resort gate at nine a.m.? My mom will call your parents to make sure it's okay."

Lizzie stormed over to the seesaw, shooing a few ghosts in her path. "Lobo!" she roared. "Seesaw with me!"

Lobo sighed and trudged over to the seesaw and took a seat. Lizzie jumped on the other side as hard as she could, launching Lobo halfway across the neighborhood.

Vlad and Gilly hit the buzzer at the gate of Jagged Rocks at 8:59 a.m. The gate buzzed and creaked open, and Elise came running out from a small yellow building just inside.

"Welcome! Come on in!"

Vlad smiled and adjusted his captain's hat. "Thanks for having us, Elise. We're looking forward to enjoying all that Jagged Rocks has to offer. Say, could you point me to the gentlemen's changing rooms, followed by the nearest waterslide?"

"Let's go say hi to my mom first," said Elise.

"Yes, of course," said Vlad. "And what shall I call the owner of this fine place?"

"You can call her Madame Delfín."

Elise led Gilly and Vlad into the front office. A tall, red-haired witch with a clipboard and a walkie-talkie stood at a desk, shuffling stacks of papers. A blue-black raven perched nearby. The witch scribbled on her clipboard and glanced at the raven. "Moose, I told you *three times* to order more mackerel for the dolphins. Now we're out, and all we have for them is catfish. They're threatening to quit, Moose. Call the harbormaster and get some mackerel. And some octopus. Now."

The raven tapped his tiny headset. "Bonjour, Karla," said Moose in a deep French accent. "We have a fish emergency at the Jagged Rocks. I'm on my way down to you now." Moose tapped his headset again and flew out the window.

"Hey, Mom! This is Vlad and Gilly."

"Enchanted, Madame Delfín," said Vlad, tipping his hat.

The witch looked up from

her work and smiled. "Hi, kids. Vlad, what a stylish little captain's hat. And, Gilly, you . . ." The witch gasped and stood up sharply. She lowered her eyes and touched her hand to her heart. "Elise, you didn't tell me that your classmate is the . . . the spawn of an Ancient Nether-Being."

Elise looked at Gilly, then back at her mom. "A what, now?"

Elise's mom looked at Gilly. "It is *such* an honor, Gilly. Such an honor."

Gilly shrugged. "Thank . . . ye." She knew that her mom

was super old and called herself a queen of "the under/inner cosmos," but Gilly usually didn't think much about it.

"How about a quick tour?" offered Elise's mom. "Then you kids can have a swim."

"Sounds great, Mom," said Elise.

Madame Delfín showed the kids the grotto, the spa, and the restaurant. Each building in the resort was made of wavy pale yellow walls and was topped with messes of curvy red tiles. The windows were a mix of circles, half circles, and crescent slivers in all sizes.

Everywhere the group went, witches gasped and bowed when they saw Gilly. On their way to the theater, three beautiful, flowy sea hags approached with their eyes lowered. They reached out to place a wreath of seaweed around Gilly's neck, then spoke in unison. "Please tell your mother (may she reign eternal) that the Coven of Cob-Derry sends its highest regards."

Vlad stepped forward. "Yeah, my parents are pretty ancient, too. My dad's, like, two hundred."

"This is such a trea-sured experience," said the sea hags. They walked backward for a few steps, then turned and skipped away.

"I be confused," said Gilly. "Why do ye all know who mine mother be?"

Madame Delfín chuckled. "There isn't a sea sorceress, swamp hag, or bog witch who doesn't love and honor your mother. Or at least fear her. Look."

Elise's mom pulled her necklace out from beneath her cloak. It was dotted with crys-tals and held a triangular silver pendant with a carved portrait of a sour-faced, five-

trunked beast
slithering out of the water.

"Aye," said Gilly. "That be her. Bizarre."

Madame Delfín touched the pendant to her forehead and tucked it back into her cloak. "Having you here is something we will never forget."

Moose swooped out of the sky and landed on his boss's shoulder. "And it will be great for business, no?" he said. "We should take a photo for the catalog."

"Get outta here, Moose!" hissed Madame Delfín. "Unless you've got good news for me."

"The . . . er . . . fish is on its way," said Moose.

"Okay, kids, I'll leave you to it. Have a swim, get something to eat. There's a team of dolphin acrobats visiting from Hawaii who will be doing a show in the theater at two p.m. Have fun! Send up a flare if you need me."

Elise's mom muttered a quick protection spell over the kids and scuttled off with Moose.

Gilly and Elise swam and talked for a couple of hours. They were interrupted a few times by witches offering Gilly little tokens or asking her to bless their crystals. Vlad wasn't loving the lack of attention he was receiving, especially with his perfectly stylish captain's hat, so he spent the morning alone at the spa. But then he discovered that showing up at the resort with Gilly had earned him a bit of a reputation, so he milked that for all it was worth: mud bath, manicure, plasma smoothie.

At noon the kids met at the restaurant, where a row of chefs and servers delivered a crusted, buttered serpent on a bed of sea cucumbers and kelp. Vlad ordered a bottle of sparkling O negative "for the table," but he was the only one who had any. A few employees of the resort rushed over and began fanning Gilly with large brown leaves. Gilly sighed and buried her face in her hands, and Elise shooed the devotees away.

"You can fan me if you want," called Vlad. They didn't answer. "Sheesh, Gilly. I don't get you. I'd have these people carrying me around on a throne."

"Ye be not me, and I be not ye."

"Well, I'm just saying. *Ye* should try to enjoy it a little."

After lunch the kids wandered around a bit. Gilly stayed between Vlad and Elise and avoided eye contact with her admirers. They peeked into the portal to the underworld, but—of course—they didn't go in. Not even Lizzie would jump through a portal to the underworld without adult supervision.

At 1:45, they headed to the theater but saw that the show had been canceled. Apparently there wasn't any mackerel at the harbor, and the sea bass that was offered made the dolphins leave in a huff.*

---

* HAWAIIAN DOLPHIN ACROBATS ARE *VERY* DEMANDING. THEY'RE DEFINITELY WORTH IT, SO IF YOU'RE BOOKING THEM FOR A PERFORMANCE, MAKE SURE YOU HAVE YOUR CONTRACT IN ORDER. ALSO, IF SOMEONE YOU KNOW IS LOOKING FOR A JOB IN THE HOSPITALITY INDUSTRY, THE OWNER OF JAGGED ROCKS RESORT, SPA, AND PORTAL TO THE UNDERWORLD IS LOOKING FOR A NEW ASSISTANT.

Gilly watched as groups of witches read the sign about the canceled show and walked away, disappointed. She ripped the sign off the entrance and pulled Vlad and Elise through the gate.

"What are you doing?" asked Elise.

"The show must go on."

Gilly waded into the water at the edge of the pool. A few clusters of witches who were lounging in the stands whispered curiously to each other.

Gilly took a deep breath and let out an otherworldly shriek that echoed through

the resort. Vlad hissed and leapt into Elise's arms.

"How did you . . . ?" asked Vlad.

Gilly shrugged.

The theater began to fill with witches. Elise looked up and saw her mom peek out of the control booth. Elise gave her mother a slightly confused nod, and Madame Delfín began pressing buttons. Lights swirled around the pool, and a thunderous beat blasted through the speakers.

Gilly put her hands in the water and muttered under her breath. The water rippled, then rocked with movement beneath the surface.

Thirteen long glowing eels burst out of the water and swam in a circle. The witches clapped in anticipation. As Gilly chanted, the eels leapt into the air and slithered into different shapes and formations.

Madame Delfín kept the lights swirling

and the music whooshing, and the audience was clapping, cheering, and dancing in the aisles.

Gilly looked up at Vlad, who was awestruck at the power of his friend. "Be you ready? 'Tis time for the star performance."

Gilly pointed at Vlad and motioned to the center of the pool.

"Me?" asked Vlad.

"Ye," replied Gilly.

Vlad nervously swam out into the water. Madame Delfín lowered the lights and the volume of the music. The eels swam in a circle around Vlad. One eel broke formation and swam a little closer. The circle became a spiral, winding tighter and tighter. The theater pool became a massive whirlpool with Vlad at the center.

At the peak of the frenzy, the water rose in a cone, lifting Vlad higher and higher. The music grew louder and louder. Suddenly,

the eels collided and burst the cone of water. Vlad was launched into the air. He lifted his hat in a salute, flipped, and dove back into the water. Then everything was quiet and still. Gilly lifted her hands out of the water and faced the crowd. Their stunned silence gave way to uproarious cheers. Several witches shot sparks and fireworks out of their wands. Vlad stood at the edge closest to the crowd and bowed. And bowed. And bowed some more.

After a relaxing afternoon in the lazy river, followed by catfish sandwiches under a secluded waterfall, it was time for Vlad and Gilly to go home.

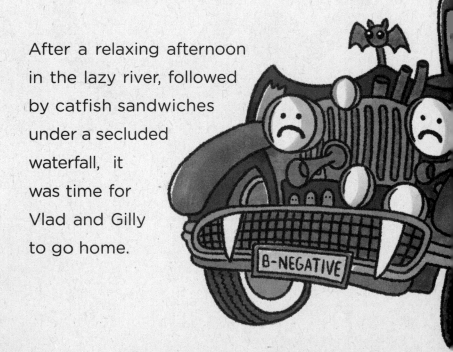

Vlad's dad arrived in the family hearse and stepped out to say hello to Madame Delfín. "Looks like I'm picking up as many kids as I dropped off, so it seems we all had a good time, yes?"

"The kids were great," said Elise's mom. "Please tell Gilly's mother (may her shrieks echo through the universe until the end of time) that it was so very special having

her here. And if there's anything at all she needs, we are at her service."

"Okaaay . . . ," said Vlad's dad.

"And, Vlad, again, what a sweet little captain's hat." Elise's mom gave Vlad a salute. Vlad blushed.

As Gilly and Vlad rode off, Elise turned

to her left and smiled. "And what about you, Griff? Did you have a nice time?"

"Yes," said Griff. "I mean no. I mean . . . I'm not here."

Elise laughed. "I can't see *you,* but I *can* see the kelp in your teeth." Elise waved as Griff's invisible feet raced away, pressing footprints in the dirt path.

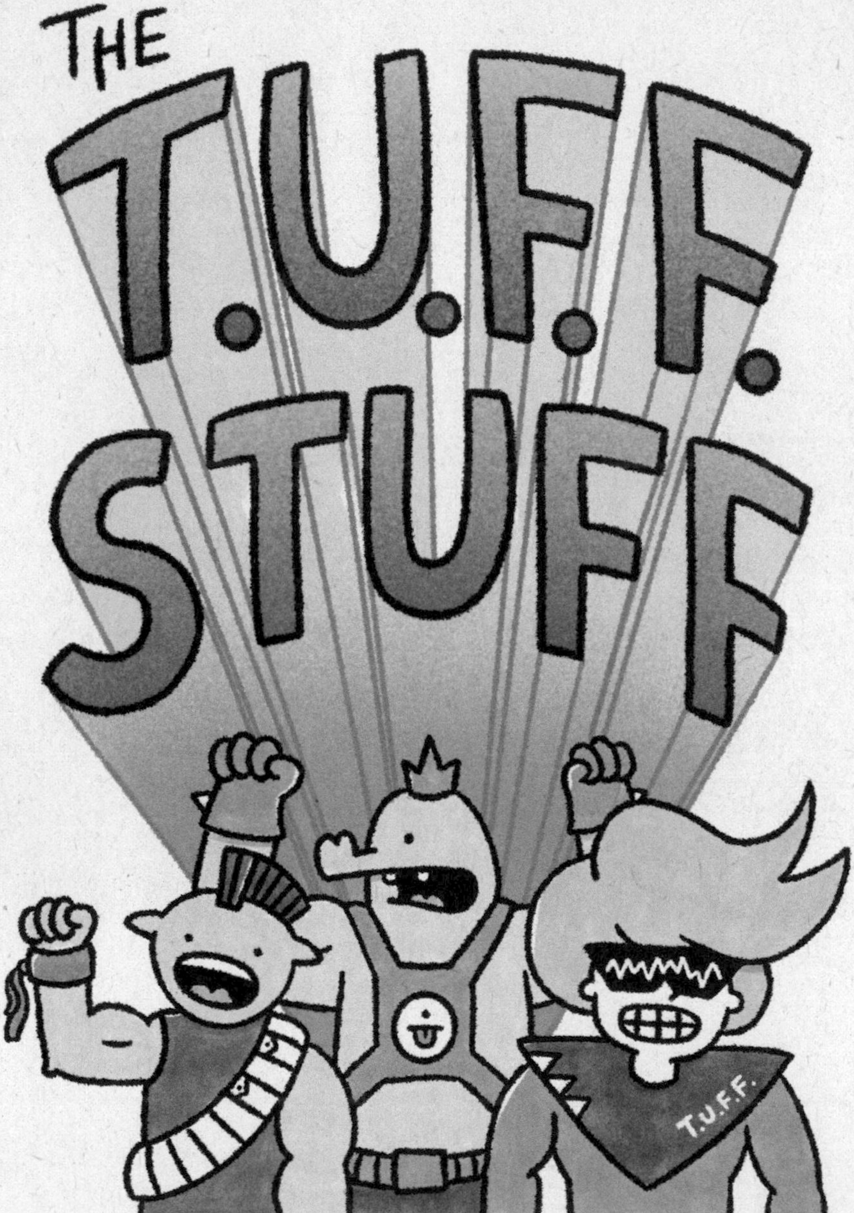
THE
T.U.F.F.
STUFF
T.U.F.F.

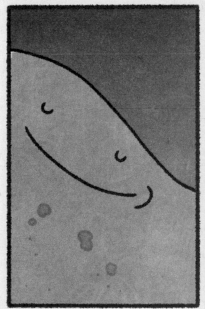

To the T.U.F.F. Battle Rocket!

Meteor, prepare to be punched!

YEAH!

C'mon, C-15k.

87

That's it. T.U.F.F. Squad! Let's show this villain what it means to have the T.U.F.F. Stuff!

Hey! That's my doll!

We're just borrowing it for a little bit.

No! MOMMM!

That's not... like you, Serpentiffany. Surely you want to battle us.

No, I just want a hug from the dinosaur man.

Dino Rusty doesn't *hug villains!*

Okay, then. Bye-bye!

95

97

There's the meteor!

Activate T.U.F.F. Puncher!

POP

THE COOL KIDS

Frankie hadn't been alive for long, but her list of scientific accomplishments was *very* impressive. Chemistry, experimental biology, evil geology, physics, theoretical horticulture—she loved it all. She loved the research, the experiments, and the discoveries. Whether she was tracing an infestation back to patient zero, growing fresh produce in the gloomiest place on earth, stitching a bunch of spare parts together and bringing them to life, or saving the entire island from an ever-expanding glob of goo, Frankie knew that science was her passion, her future, and the solution to any problem.

Frankie was excited all morning about her class's upcoming science experiment, "Which worm has the worst attitude?" She sharpened five pencils until they were so pointy that they could split atoms, and she had a brand-new notebook ready to go. The tray of worms was waiting on a worktable, and she had already begun to form a

hypothesis when she should have been fo-
cusing on the Dead Languages lesson.

"Step 1: State the hypothesis." Frankie
looked at the diagram she had sketched
when she first got to class. "Worm #5 has
the worst attitude. It's turned away from
the other worms. Step 2: Assumptions. If
Worm #5 is isolated, it will begin to understand that—"

THWACK! Ms. Verne smacked a tentacle
next to Frankie's chair.

"Sorry, Ms. Verne."

"Ω◊i•⧨‡ ∞Σå æŒΠʃʃ৭. ¶μ⌣ᵦ£. ৎ∆ʃ
Ẍ⅄ʊ☺∆æ."

"Wow . . . really?"

"ᴙΣ•¶⧨∞Ô Σ'i† ⁻°æ⧨ ʊ˄∞Σ´∞."

Frankie put her notebook in her desk
and looked at the hieroglyphs on the chalkboard. She wouldn't be able to test her hypothesis, but what she'd be doing instead
was even more exciting.

"Science class at Triple M? That's epic." Griff tried to jump and grab a branch, but he missed and fell on the ground. Nobody noticed.

Triple M was what Griff (and no one else) called Madame Muggy Middle School, which was across the swamp field from Stubtoe Elementary.

"They're all so *grown up* and cool," said Quade.

"Are you nervous?" asked Elise.

"I guess not," said Frankie. "I'm curious about the projects I'll be doing."

"You need to focus, Frankie," said Vlad. "This is an opportunity. Better parties, more mature convos. You gotta put in a good word for me."

"No way," porfed Bobby. "She's not going to want to hang out with us anymore. She'll be too busy discussing businesses or what-ever."

"I bet they stay up *so* late," said Erik. "Look at them."

The kids turned toward the side of the field where the Muggy Middle kids hung out at recess. There was a banshee, a couple of centaurs, a werewolf, a ghost, a boogeykid, a chupacabra, and a handful of other kids who Frankie and her friends were equal parts scared of and in awe of.

Allie wiped the fog from her helmet. "Begin.Transmission . . . They.Are.So.
Majestic . . . End.Transmission."

"COOOOOOOOL," agreed Emma.

"Be ye worried about them liking ye?" asked
Gilly.

"I really haven't thought about it," said
Frankie.

"You should think about it," Griff said. "You should think about it a lot."

A flash of light caught the kids' attention. They looked toward Madame Muggy Middle School to see lightning strike the dark, crumbling bell tower. The building was made of patchy stucco, and most of the windows were boarded up. The drawbridge was lit on either side by oily torches. There was a faint scream from somewhere inside.

Lizzie chuckled. "Nice knowing you."

Ms. Verne rang the bell to end recess.

"Okay, Frankie," said Quade. "This is it. I know it's going to go great."

"Thanks," said Frankie. She grabbed her notebook and pencils from her desk. "I'll see you all after."

"Whoa, whoa, whoa," said Griff. "What do you think you're doing?"

Frankie was puzzled. "Going to Muggy Middle, remember?"

"Not with that, you aren't," said Griff. "And I'm pointing at your notebook."

Frankie looked at her notebook cover. "What's wrong with it?"

Lizzie groaned. "*Snail Pals*? You can't go over there with a *Snail Pals* notebook. They'll eat you alive if they see that baby stuff."

"I like *Snail Pals*," said Frankie. "Great theme song, too. *Home is where your heart, liver, and kidney are.*"

Quade sang the next line with her. *"I'm always home, and you're always hoooome with meeee."* They laughed together.

"This is going to be a disaster," said Vlad. "Lobo, back me up. You have an older sister. What is she into? What does she like?"

Lobo shrugged. "I have no idea. Every once in a while, I knock on her door, and she yells *WHAT?* and I say *Hi, Grita, it's me,* and she yells *WHAT DO YOU WANT?* and I say *I'm just saying hi,* and she yells *WELL, YOU'VE SAID IT, NOW GO BUG SOME-BODY ELSE.* That's pretty much our whole thing."

"See," said Vlad. "That's it right there. No chitchat. No nonsense. No sugarcoating."

"Vlad's right," said Griff. "Older kids are into creepoball, cars, and films. Not movies. *Films.*"

"Well, *now* I'm really nervous," said Frankie. "Thanks, everyone." She tore the front cover off her notebook and left the classroom.

"Δ̇÷Ω≈©. ꝼꝺ ſſåꝺ ſ̃μ£ꝕ ꝕ•ꞔ."

Frankie waved shyly and sat at a table between a handsome centaur with long brown hair and a flickering ghost with a melty face. In the center of the table, a silent robot sat next to a tray containing a lump of pinkish meat with a bunch of tubes sticking out.

"Hi," said Frankie.

"Hey," said the centaur. "Hector."

"Tabby," cried the ghost. "Woooooo-ooooh."

"You're that kid who blew up the huge glob in the last book, right?" asked Hector.

"Yes," said Frankie, "that was me."

"Coooooo-ooooool," wailed Tabby.

"So we're building a heart for a robot,"

said Hector, pointing at the tray of artificial gore. "But we can't get the aorta to fit right."

Frankie prodded at the heart. "Hmm . . ."

"Any ideas?" asked Hector.

"Oh!" Frankie flipped the largest tube around and popped it into the lump. "You just had it backward. No problem."

The heart began pumping. "Nice one, Frankie!" cheered Hector. He lifted the heart out of the tray and clicked it into the body of the robot, which whirred and beeped and opened its eyes.

Frankie sang under her breath, *"Home is where your heart, liver, and kidney are."*

"I'm always home," sang Hector and Tabby, *"and you're always hoooome with meeee."*

The rest of the big kids turned and stared. Hector, Tabby, and Frankie laughed.

"Snail Pals was the beeeee's kneeeees," sobbed Tabby. "I wonder if it's still on."

"Tabs, you know *good and well* that it's still on," said Hector.

"Yeah, you got me."

Hector sighed. "I wish I had a shell I could curl up into."

"Really?" asked Frankie. "I think you're . . . majestic."

"I know," said Hector. "But not as majestic as a Snail Pal."

"None of us are," said the robot.

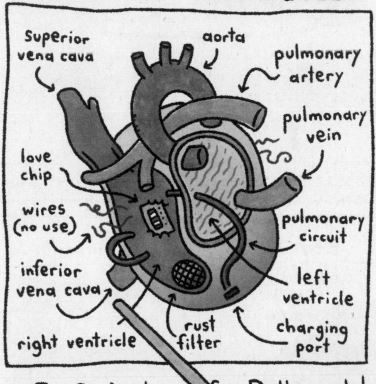

Frankie presents...
SCIENCE CHUNKS

superior vena cava

aorta

pulmonary artery

pulmonary vein

love chip

wires (no use)

inferior vena cava

pulmonary circuit

left ventricle

right ventricle

rust filter

charging port

Fig. 2. Anatomy of a Delta model robo-bio heart

Lasers.

Um... lightning.

Oh! Lightning!

Fire.

120

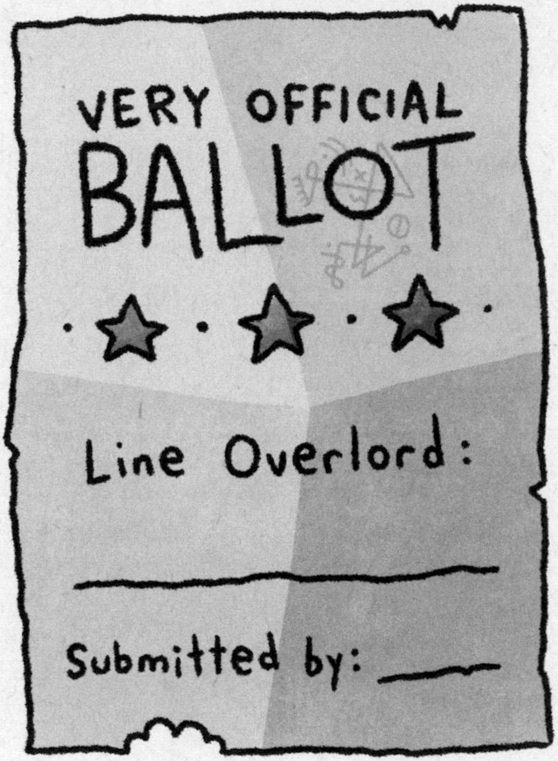
VERY OFFICIAL
BALLOT
Line Overlord:
Submitted by:

ELECTION DAY

Each month, the older-ish class at Stub-toe Elementary had an election for a new Line Overlord. It's the Line Overlord's job to line up the class and lead the way to and from the cafeteria. The Line Overlord also helps Ms. Verne clean the chalkboard, catch and release pixies that come in through open windows, and do other little jobs here and there.

On the first Monday of the month, everyone interested in running for Line Overlord would write their names on the chalkboard sometime before lunch. Then, following afternoon free time, a silent election would be held.

For several months, Quade's name was the only one written on the board. The kids generally agreed that Quade did a good job, was always nice to everyone, and was tall enough to reach the top of the chalkboard when standing on a chair.

When election time came around one Monday and the kids were filing into the classroom, Elise, who hadn't been around

for a Line Overlord election before, asked why Quade's name was on the board. When she heard the story, she asked why no one else ever ran against him.

"Why anyone would want the job is beyond me," said Erik. "But he's decent enough at it. Watch me shrug." Erik shrugged.

"Yeah, and he's really nice," said Frankie. "That's a good quality for a Line Overlord."

"Begin.Transmission . . . Agreed . . . End. Transmission," said Allie.

"Plus, why would anyone want to try to get extra chores?" asked Vlad.

"I guess that all makes sense," said Elise. "But an actual election could be fun."

Lizzie gasped. **"I HEREBY ANNOUNCE THAT I AM RUNNING FOR LINE OVERLORD,"** she declared. Lizzie pounded up to the chalkboard and added her name.

Bobby hurgled and slurfed. "Elise, do you have any idea what you have done?"

Vlad, Emma, Gilly, and Frankie huddled together in the reading nook. "If Lizzie becomes Line Overlord, we're doomed," whispered Frankie.

"DOOOOOOOOOMED," groaned Emma.

"We simply must vote for Quade," offered Gilly. "There be no problem."

"It's not that simple," said Vlad. "If there's a landslide victory, Lizzie will freak out."

"Too true," said Frankie. "We need a coordinated effort so it's close, but also not too close. Can't risk it."

"RIIIIIIIIIISK," groaned Emma.

Vlad started taking a head count. "We just need to tell the others to make sure to— Wait, what's Lobo doing?"

Lobo was standing at the chalkboard. He stepped away, revealing that he had written his name on the list of candidates for Line Overlord. He walked over to Lizzie in the art station. They high-foured.

"Wait—what is happening?" asked Vlad.

"Bad news, guys," said Griff.

"Griff, where are you?" asked Frankie.

An invisible hand tapped Frankie on the shoulder. "I'm right here. And I've got terrible news. You're not gonna believe this. Okay. *Lobo is running for Line Overlord.*"

"WEEEE KNOOOOW," groaned Emma.

"But why is Lizzie happy about it?" asked Vlad.

Griff threw his hands up. Nobody saw. "She told him he should run. That it would show everyone how responsible and loyal and good he is."

"She's . . . she's splitting up the 'nice' vote," said Frankie. "Brilliant. Evil, but brilliant."

"We must tell the others before it be too late," declared Gilly.

Ms. Verne slapped a tentacle on the chalkboard. "Σø^¥ss å≤∞ƒ." It was too late.

128

Quade brought a box from the cloak closet and placed it on Ms. Verne's desk. Then he passed out little slips of paper to everyone, whispering *good luck* to Lobo and Lizzie.

Vlad and Frankie glanced at each other in silent panic. One by one, the kids dropped their voting slips into the box. When the votes were all in, Ms. Verne unfolded them one by one and wrote hash marks next to the names on the board.

One vote for Quade.

One vote for Lizzie.

One vote for Quade.

One vote for Lobo.

One vote for Lobo.

One vote for Lizzie.

One vote for Lizzie.

This can't be happening, thought Vlad.

What beautiful chaos, thought Erik.

One vote for Lobo.

Wow! thought Lobo. *Three whole votes! I can't wait to tell Mom and Dad!*

One vote for Quade.

One vote for Lizzie.

One vote for Quade.

Lizzie and Quade are tied, thought Frankie. *This is it.*

One vote . . . for Lizzie.

Lizzie leapt up and roared. "I **DID IT!** Check me out, bestie! I am the **CHAMPION!**"

"Nice," said Elise. "See, I told you all how much fun an election could be."

Lizzie snarled. "There's gonna be some **CHANGES** around here."

The class was silent and sullen. Ms. Verne broke the tension with a joke. "#∫œΣ ô˙Δº¬ Ω≈åi£¢ ¢•." Everyone except for Erik laughed for a solid ten seconds.

"What's wrong, Erik?" jorgled Bobby.

Erik looked around the room. "Am I . . . the only one who doesn't understand a single word Ms. Verne says?"

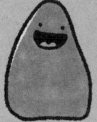

GOO BOATS

One of my favorite snacks is a couple of GOO BOATS. They're super customizable and fun to make. GO!

STEP 1: CHOOSE YOUR BOAT!

celery
long & stringy

cucumber
sliced & scooped

bell pepper
holds the most stuff

Have an adult help with any knife stuff! Be aware of food allergies!

STEP 2: CHOOSE YOUR GOO & FILL YOUR BOAT!

hummus

cream cheese

peanut butter

STEP 3: CHOOSE YOUR PASSENGERS! SPRINKLE & PRESS!

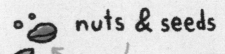 nuts & seeds

dried and/or fresh fruit

roasted grubs

TERRIBLE CHOICES:
THE SLEEPOVER

This story is full of choices that *you* get to make. You'll find options along the way, and you'll be asked to flip to different pages based on your decisions (rather than reading straight through). There are EIGHT different endings (no peeking!), so when you reach one, flip back to this page and see how else your story might go. Now . . . make some *TERRIBLE CHOICES* in this adventure: The Sleepover.

You were born in a rotting landfill in Oregon. You and your family are wereskunks. You know, like werewolves, but smellier and arguably cooler-looking. Humans tend to freak out about monsters *and* skunks, so you have to hide who you are. Your only friends in the dump are seagulls and rats, and finally your parents decide to move to Creep's Cove for a better life.

Now you're the new kid at Stubtoe Elementary, and you're quickly making lots of friends. It's going so well that you get invited to sleep over at Allie's house and Griff's house on the same night. What should you do?

THE CHOICE IS CLEAR. SLEEP OVER AT GRIFF'S HOUSE.
(TURN TO THE NEXT PAGE.)

YOU JUST GOT HERE; SHE'S AN ALIEN. NEW KIDS, UNITE! CHOOSE ALLIE. (TURN TO PAGE 143.)

You arrive at Griff's house . . . you think. The address is on the curb, but the lot seems empty. Then you see it. The entire house is made of glass. Makes sense for an invisible family. You feel around and eventually find a doorbell. You ring it. Then you notice a pair of sunglasses bouncing down what you assume is a staircase from above and ten feet away. It's Griff!

Griff throws the door open. "Yeah! Welcome to my humble abode, chumarino! C'mon in! Oh! Erik's here!"

138

You turn around and see Erik walking up the path with his sleeping bag.

"Welcome," says a voice next to Griff. "Griff has told me so much about you. Make yourselves at home. There's jerky in the den. Help yourselves. And let me know when you kids want to order some food."

"This is gonna be the best Fri-hang ever!" declares Griff. "What should we do first?"

"LET'S PLAY A GAME, CHUMARINOS!"
(TURN TO PAGE 150.)

"LET'S GET SOME CHOW, CHUMARINOS!"
(TURN TO PAGE 142.)

139

PIZZA! PIZZA! PIZZA! The obvious choice, right?

After the order is placed, it feels like an *eternity* before the food arrives. When it does, you huddle around the boxes. You smile at each other and lift the top. All your favorite toppings are there: pickles, peppermint, popcorn, and peaches.

You grab a few slices and dig in. It's better than any pizza you found lying around the junkyard back in Oregon. You know that you're really going to enjoy living here in Creep's— Uh-oh . . .

Your stomach rumbles and flips. Oof! You feel terrible, but maybe the feeling will pass in a little— Nope. Ow.

You realize that you've got a rough night ahead of you, so you call home to get picked up. Your first sleepover on Creep's Cove was . . . pretty good, all things considered.

THE END

Griff claps and whoops. "Great idea! Let's **EAT.**"

Griff yells for his dad, and you hear footsteps and see a newspaper slowly coming toward you. "Hey, kiddos. Hungry?"

You all nod.

"Well, let's see. Sushi or pizza?"

Griff votes for pizza, and Erik votes for sushi. The tiebreaking vote is yours.

"LET'S ORDER SUSHI!" (TURN TO PAGE 147.)

"LET'S ORDER PIZZA!" (TURN TO PAGE 140.)

142

You hike up a winding, rocky hillside. As you turn a corner around a moss-covered boulder, you see it: a crashed spaceship sticking halfway out of the ground. It's Allie's house.

Allie and Emma are standing outside. They wave to you as you approach. Allie turns to a keypad and taps a long sequence. There's a hiss and a puff of steam as a panel on the ship slides up. "Begin.Transmission. This.Being.Welcomes.You.To.The.Residence. Of.This.Being.End.Transmission."

Allie motions for you and Emma to enter. She follows you in, and the door slides shut behind her. There's a keypad on the opposite wall, and she types a different sequence, even longer than the first. "Begin.Transmission.Prepare.Yourselves. For.A.Pressure.Change.And.Do.Not.Be. Alarmed.End.Transmission."

There's a slow hiss as the air inside the ship rushes into the airlock. It smells

metallic and slightly stale. Your ears pop, and you feel a little queasy for a moment, but it passes.

"WEEEEEIRD," groans Emma.

The ship is full of large machinery, most of it covered in white sheets. Little lights flicker, and there's a constant hum.

Allie takes off her helmet and hangs it on the wall. "Begin.Transmission . . . Activating. Casual.Conversation.Mode . . . Hello, friends. Let us commence the sleepover. What shall we do first?"

"COULD I TRY ON YOUR HELMET?" (TURN TO PAGE 152.)

"WAIT A SECOND. YOU CAN TALK NORMALLY?"
(TURN TO PAGE 166.)

You roll out your sleeping bag and wiggle into it. Griff flips off the light, and suddenly it feels like you're outside. Through the glass ceiling and walls you see the fullness of the dark. Bats fly overhead, lizards creep across the lawn, and trees wave and scratch against the house.

It's terrifying, and you feel completely unsafe. You lie awake for hours as every creepy thing on the island seems to be looking directly at you, longing to chomp on your bones. What little sleep you find is full of nightmares. A tragic end to an otherwise-epic Fri-hang with your new chumarinos.

THE END

Griff's dad calls in an order, then hands Griff a couple of silver coins. "Save me a few bites if you can," he says. "I'll be in my study."

You read comic books and chat for a little while, and then the doorbell rings. You look toward the front door, which you can see through the glass walls. Is that . . . Ms. Verne?

You follow Griff and Erik to the front door. Sure enough, it's Ms. Verne, and she's holding a delivery bag. "Hi, Ms. Verne," says Griff. "You . . . work at the sushi place?"

"**Ü°˜≥µå,**" says Ms. Verne. "**ŒꜰËΣ ÂÜŒΔ ÆøµiΩ≈ç√∫.**"

Griff hands her the coins and takes the bag. "Okay, see you Monday."

You breathlessly rush to Griff's dad's study. "Dad!" yells Griff. "Ms. Verne . . . the sushi . . ."

"Yes," says Griff's dad. "There are many things you don't know about Ms. Verne.

Things that would keep you up at night. Things that would . . . haunt . . . your dreams."

He grabs a few rolls from the bag and flips over his newspaper. He's lost in thought.

You run back to the den with Griff and Erik and dig in. There's so much amazing stuff! Bright, strange stuff you've never seen before. Little green pieces of stuff and big orange pieces of stuff wrapped in rice and seaweed. Scaly stuff, feathery stuff. Soup with squeaky chunks of stuff. Soon you're stuffed with stuff.

"Wow," says Griff. "That was epic. What should we do now?"

"We could watch some music videos," says Erik. "I made a playlist."

You know that Erik has gloomy taste in music, and you're pretty sleepy, so maybe it's time to call it a night. What do you think?

"ACTUALLY, I'M GONNA TURN IN. WHAT A NIGHT!"
(TURN TO PAGE 146.)

"THE NIGHT IS YOUNG. CUE THE MUSIC!"
(TURN TO PAGE 167.)

149

"You know Griff, and if you know Griff, and I know you do, you know that Griff loooooooooves games," says Griff. Griff runs down a clear hallway, opens a clear door, and pulls out a . . . (whew!) thankfully *not-clear* box.

"Friends, I give you . . . *Kozmo-Beeests of Planet Gulbatron*!"

"It looks complicated," says Erik.

"You'll get the hang of it pretty quickly," replies Griff. He sets out a game board, a thick book, a bunch of dice, a spinner, an hourglass, and a dozen different figurines. "Okay, so welcome to Gulbatron. I will be your game master and guide. First, roll these three dice."

You roll the dice and listen to Griff read a long introductory passage about the game. You pick up a piece of jerky from a bowl. The label says GRIFF FAMILY JERKY and promises A TASTE THAT'S FAR FROM INVISIBLE. You take a bite. It's not like any jerky you've had before, but it's pretty good!

Griff tries to walk you through the rules and playing instructions, but the game is super complicated. It barely makes sense.

OH, JUST GO FOR IT. IT'LL BE FUN. (TURN TO PAGE 155.)

"CAN WE . . . PLAY SOMETHING ELSE?" (TURN TO PAGE 161.)

A game of dress-up," says Allie. "Agreed. Exchange articles." She hands you her helmet and cape. You put them on and feel like a fish in a bowl. Emma drapes Allie in a spare roll of wraps, then pulls a sheet over herself.

"GHOOOOOOOST."

Allie makes a clucking sound that is probably supposed to sound like a laugh. She presses a button on a console and leans toward a panel next to it. "Guardian, I request your presence at the helm."

There's a long beep from overhead, and a screen drops from the ceiling. It clicks on, and the face of a huge bug-eyed alien with a pulsating brain appears.

"Begin.Transmission.Greetings.Spawn. And.Companions.Of.Spawn.It.Appears. That.You.Are.Engaging.In.An.Act. Of.Amusement.End.Transmission."

"Greetings, Guardian," says Allie. "You are correct. We have altered our garments.

Would you comply with documenting this moment?"

"Begin.Transmission.This.Being.Complies. Pose.Yourselves.End.Transmission."

You stand next to Emma and Allie and put your hands on your hips. There's a room-filling flash that makes you see spots for a few minutes. Three photos whir out of a nearby slot.

"That was an amusing moment," says Allie. "Let us continue with the consumption of foodstuffs. Do you comply?"

"LET'S ORDER SOME PIZZA!" (TURN TO PAGE 140.)

"LET'S ORDER FROM MOGWAI'S WOK!" (TURN TO PAGE 164.)

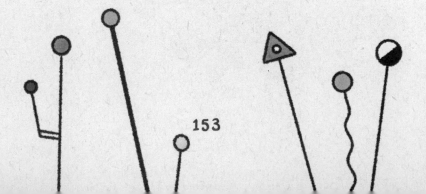

153

You watch and listen, and you begin to see what Erik loves about it. It's **REAL**. It's raw. It's powerful. An hour later, the three of you are crying and singing along at the tops of your lungs. You keep it going until the edge of the horizon begins to turn gray. You pass out on the floor next to your two new best chumarinos, happier than you knew you could be, way out in the middle of the fish-stinking ocean on Creep's Cove.

THE END

You get comfortable with only sort of knowing what's going on. Griff does a good job
of walking you through (you check the box
to confirm the title) Kozmo-Beeests of
Planet Gulbatron. You're an intergalactic
adventurer gathering pieces of a legendary
amulet across a dozen planets. Griff tells
you and Erik what you need to do along the
way, like when to roll the dice, what planets
you should visit, and what you need before
facing different Kozmo-Beeests.

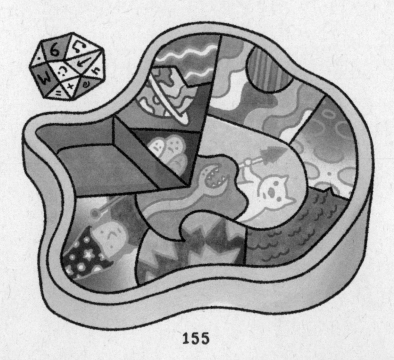

You play for hours. Finally you and Erik find the last piece of the amulet and win the game. You won! Somehow! So you're told! Epic!

"THAT WAS GREAT. SHOULD WE GET SOMETHING TO EAT?" (TURN TO PAGE 159.)

ASK ERIK WHAT HE WANTS TO DO NEXT.
(TURN TO PAGE 167.)

Griff pulls a board aside, and you slip through the opening. You find yourself in a foggy swamp. You hear croaking in the distance—primo toad territory indeed! You run as fast as you can toward the sound, then suddenly find yourselves falling, falling, falling . . . then splashing into the bottom of a muddy pit.

It's pitch-black, it's full of bugs, and it smells terrible. "Oh," says Griff. "So this is why I'm not allowed back here."

The three of you yell at the top of your lungs, but no one hears you. You spend all night in the pit, covered in muck. Finally, as the sky grows a little lighter, you hear a voice.

"Griff? Kids? Are you down there?" Griff's dad finds you! He drops a rope ladder, and you make your way back to the surface.

It's a rough end to a decent Fri-hang, and once Griff isn't grounded anymore, maybe you can have him over at your place—a house with walls you can't see through and a backyard swamp without a dangerous, filthy pit.

THE END

Griff squints at the see-through clock and somehow makes out the time. "Whoa!" he says. "It's too late to order anything. Let's raid the kitchen."

Griff lays out six slices of bread on the counter, turns to you and Erik, and says, "Artists, here are your canvases."

You, Erik, and Griff smile at each other and open the fridge and the pantry. You load up your sandwich with peanut butter, ketchup, cold noodles, dried apples, and pickled onions. It's . . . so . . . good. You share bites with your friends and argue about whose sandwich is the best.

You feast and laugh and talk until you can't keep your eyes open for another second. You fall asleep with crumbs and a smile on your face, the happiest wereskunk in Creep's Cove.

THE END

"I'm sorry, Griff," you say. "But could we maybe play something else?"

"No problemo!" says Griff. "Let's go out and look for toads. My dad's company will buy them from us."

"What for, Griff?" you ask.

"For their products," says Griff.

"Your dad's . . . jerky company?" you ask.

"Yep," says Griff.

You grab flashlights and tiptoe into the backyard. You search for an hour or so, but you don't find any toads.

"Yeah, I might have caught all the ones nearby," says Griff. "We can check the swamp past the fence. I haven't looked out there yet."

"IT'S PROBABLY PRIMO TOAD TERRITORY!"
(TURN TO PAGE 157.)

"AH, LET'S GO INSIDE AND GET SOMETHING TO EAT."
(TURN TO PAGE 159.)

"Ah, yes," says Allie. "The consumption of food. A required staple of an earthling sleepover."

"FOOOOOOOOD," agrees Emma.

"Then it is settled," says Allie. "Shall we order something, or would you prefer to try some food from my home world?"

YOU HAVE A BIT OF A SENSITIVE STOMACH. "LET'S PLAY IT SAFE AND ORDER SOMETHING." (TURN TO THE NEXT PAGE.)

YOU LOVE TRYING NEW THINGS. "LET'S EAT SOMETHING FROM YOUR HOME PLANET!" (TURN TO PAGE 172.)

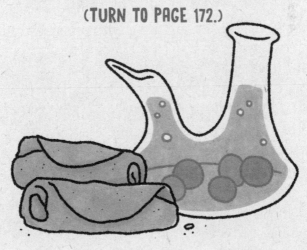

Emma talks about egg rolls all the time, and you know her favorite place is Mogwai's Wok, so you make a suggestion. Allie taps an order into a tablet, and in twenty minutes a bell rings. A screen lights up with a view outside the ship. A majestic centaur wearing a hat and vest and holding a large paper bag huffs impatiently at the door.

Allie takes control of a joystick, and a claw extends toward the centaur. The centaur looks puzzled for a moment, then holds out

the bag. Allie taps a button on the joystick, and the claw snatches the bag. She taps another button, and a chunk of purple crystal pops out and hits the centaur in the chest. He catches it, inspects it, nods, and turns to leave. Allie draws the claw back into the ship.

Dinner is served. The food is gooooood. You eat, eat, and eat a little more. Soon you're full and sleepy. Is it bedtime already?

ROLL OUT YOUR SLEEPING BAG AND SNOOZE.
(TURN TO PAGE 170.)

FIGHT YOUR SLEEPINESS. THE NIGHT IS YOUNG!
(TURN TO PAGE 168.)

"Indeed," says Allie. "Using the extra power reserves of this ship, I can activate a program that allows for more refined speech. I'm told my usual way of talking is somewhat difficult to parse."

"Oh, nonono," you say. "We can all understand you just fine."

"Excellent," says Allie. "So, what shall we do first?"

"CAN I TRY ON YOUR HELMET?" (TURN TO PAGE 152.)

"GOT ANYTHING TO EAT?" (TURN TO PAGE 163.)

166

Erik pulls a little tablet out of his backpack and loads up some music videos. The first song is slow and sad and ends with footage of tears falling into a bucket for five minutes. The second song is slower and sadder than the first. Erik is swaying to the music. You're not sure how much more of this you can take.

OH, GIVE IT A CHANCE. (TURN TO PAGE 154.)

ENOUGH OF THAT. IT'S BEDTIME. (TURN TO PAGE 146.)

167

Allie and Emma roll out their sleeping bags and lie down, but you don't want the night to end just yet. You grab a book and your flashlight from your backpack and pull your sleeping bag over your head. You're only reading for a few minutes in your squishy, private cave when you hear Emma snoring. You cover your mouth to stifle a laugh.

You hear shuffling next to you. You peek out and see Allie leaving the room. You listen through the hum of the ship, and you start to make out three voices. You slip out of your sleeping bag and tiptoe to the doorway.

Peering around the corner, you see Allie talking to her guardian and another enormous alien. The guardians speak in unison. "Begin.Transmission . . . It.Is.Agreed . . . These.Beings.Will.Commence.The.Attack. On.This.World.In.Three.Days . . . End.Transmission."

Allie nods. "Agreed. This planet is ours."

You gasp in shock. The three aliens turn and see you. A guardian shoots out a metal tentacle and grabs your arm, drawing you into the room.

"Begin.Transmission . . . This.Being.Has. Heard.Too.Much . . . It.Must.Not.Leave."

"Sorry, chumarino," says Allie.

END TRANSMISSION

You fall asleep. When you wake up, fully rested, there's the smell of something cooking. You get up and walk to the next room and see Allie's guardian pouring batter on a metal panel. A stack of steaming foot-wide pancakes sits on a platter.

"Begin.Transmission.This.Being.Wishes. You.A.Pleasant.Morning.End.Transmission."

"Good morning," you say.

"Begin.Transmission.This.Being. Is.Preparing.Heated.Grain.Disks.Should.You. Require.Nourishment.End.Transmission."

Allie and Emma join you in the kitchen.

"PAAAANCAAAAKES," groans Emma.

"Pleasant morning, Guardian," says Allie. She turns to you and Emma. "Pleasant morning. Let us agree that this 'sleepover' experience has come to the best possible conclusion available."

THE BEST END

You follow Allie into the next room. It's full of beakers of bubbling liquid and machines with tubes sticking out in every direction. Allie presses a large button, and a panel slides open. Three apple-sized purple balls roll out on the counter in front of you.

"Let us eat," says Allie.

Emma pokes at her "food," but you pick yours up and take a bite. It's as soft as a banana and tastes like a mix between dark chocolate and a hot dog. "Mmm," you say. But your voice sounds deeper than usual. That's weird. . . .

It feels like the ship is shaking. You realize that it's you. You look at your hands. They're swelling and lengthening. The fur is growing and changing colors.

"This is unexpected," says Allie.

"UNEXPECTED?!" you roar. Your otherworldly voice bellows through the whole ship. Your tongue bumps up against your teeth in an unfamiliar way. "Mirror!"

Allie scrambles around and finds a circular piece of metal. She holds it up to your face. You don't recognize yourself. Your once-black fur is bright pink and covered in white stripes. Two of your teeth have turned into tusks that hang below your chin. Your family is going to freak out when they see you.

You're . . . you're beautiful. Best sleepover ever.

THE END

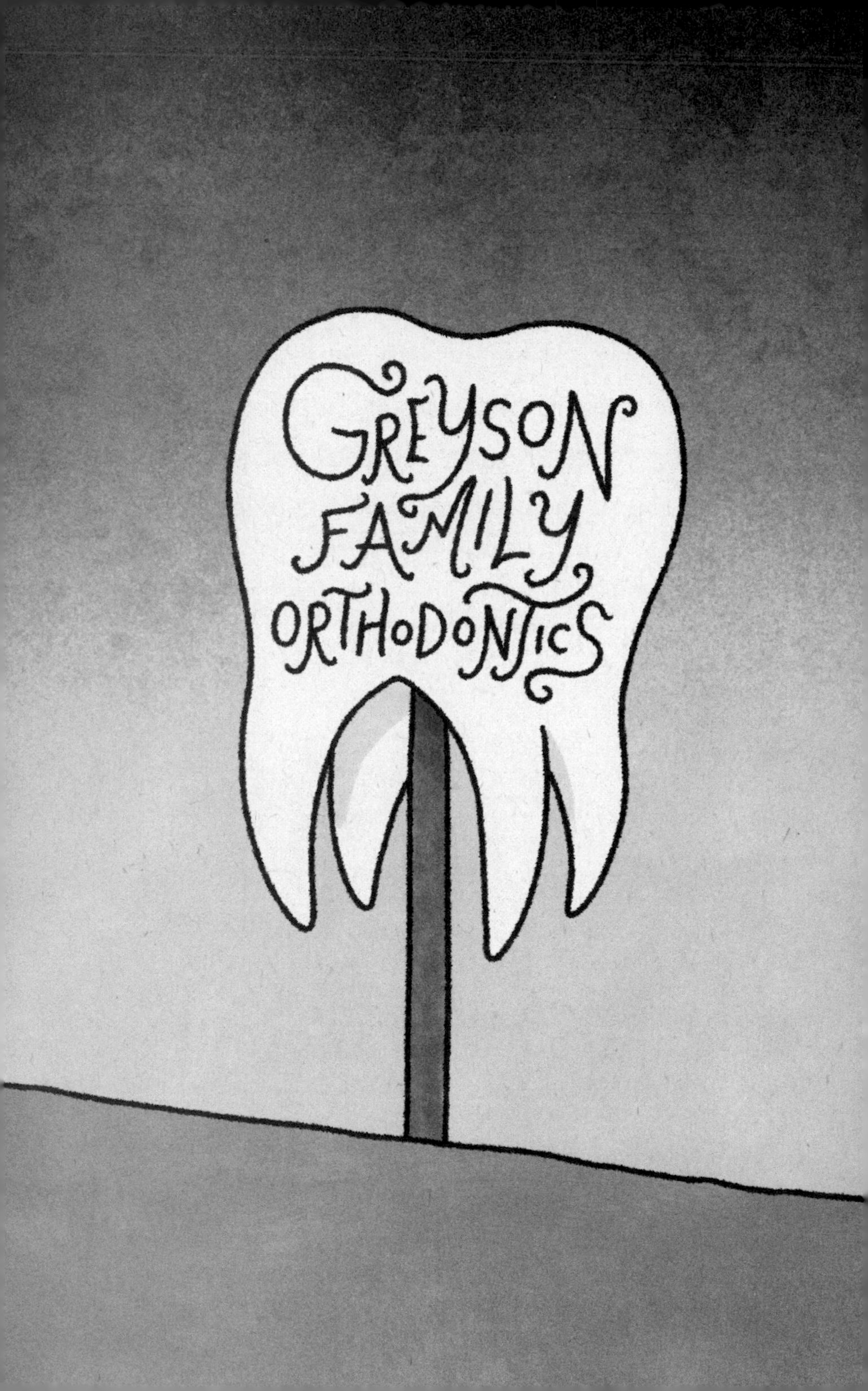
GREYSON
FAMILY
ORTHODONTICS

BRACE YOURSELVES

"This fang riiiight here is coming in just a little bit crooked." Dr. Cleara Greyson, the orthodontist on Creep's Cove, tapped her invisible finger on Vlad's top right canine tooth.

"Hmm, what do you suggest?" asked Vlad's father.

"Braces can get these neck-jabbers straightened up in a little over a year," said Dr. Greyson.

Vlad gasped and sputtered, his mouth

propped open with brass clamps. "BWAY-CETH? Ah need bwayceth?!"

"No need to worry about it, Vlad. With these braces, you won't even—"

"THITH ITH AWTHOHM!"

"Oh." Dr. Greyson chuckled. "Well, we can get you all set up tomorrow after school if that works."

"Works for me," said Vlad's dad. "Vlad?"

Vlad nodded ferociously and pounded his fists on the arms of the chair.

Bobby flerfed next to an easel holding a stack of poster boards. Vlad stood on the other side and tapped the easel with a knotted branch. Purple flames shot out from the end and scorched a nearby tree.

"OH! This isn't my presentation pointer," said Vlad.

Elise rushed over to Vlad. "Whoops! *There's* my wand." She handed Vlad a long stick. "And I'm guessing this is your presentation-pointer-thingy?"

"Ah. Yep."

Vlad tapped the easel with his presentation pointer. Purple flames did not shoot out from the end. "Gather around, friends. I have a very important announcement and presentation." He nodded at Bobby.

Bobby plorped the first piece of poster board. The card read: BRACE YOURSELVES.

"Behold!" announced Vlad. "On this very day, after school, yours truly will have bestowed upon him . . ." Vlad poked Bobby with his pointer.

Bobby plorped to the next sheet. On it was a drawing of Vlad's giant smile adorned with sparkling brackets and wires. "BRACES!"

Frankie clapped. Quade and Erik went, "Ooooh!" Emma went, "OOOOO-UUUUUGGGGGHHHHHH." Lizzie seethed with jealousy.

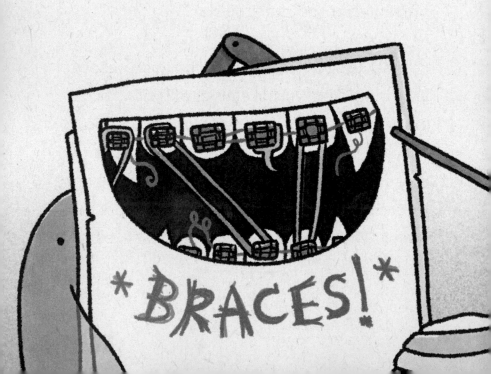

Vlad beamed. "That's right. After school, one Dr. Greyson, DDS, is installing a set of immaculate braces on these pearly whites."

"Yeah, my mom's pretty much the best orthodontist in the world," said Griff. "She did Madame Muggy's cousin's retainer."

"Oh," said Lobo. "But doesn't she—"

"Back to me," interrupted Vlad. "Anyway, as the first among you to receive such an honor, I'd like to share some rules and regulations that all of you should be aware of."

Bobby plorped to the next sheet of poster board, which read RULES AND REGULATIONS.

Vlad cleared his throat, and Bobby plorped to the next sheet, which showed a circle and

slash over braced teeth chomping down on an ear of corn.

"My braces must be protected from hard and/or sticky foods," instructed Vlad. "Keep your cobbed corn and caramelized apples *away* from me."

"Don't you only, you know, drink blood?" asked Frankie.

"Indeed," said Vlad. "And blood is safe to consume. Next slide, please."

The next sheet showed a foamy toothbrush, floss, and a cup of water. "It is very important to take good care of one's teeth and braces. After every meal, I shall be—"

NNNNNNNOPE!

"Sorry to jump in," said Quade. "But it's almost time for school, and I'm not sure this part of the presentation pertains to us all that much."

"This is crucial information," corrected Vlad. "It is important that we all—"

The bell rang, and everyone filed inside.

"We'll continue the presentation at lunch!"

Vlad's presentation stretched through the *entire* lunch hour, as well as recess and afternoon free time. He covered the history of orthodontics, the importance of dutifully attending appointments for the upkeep of braces, and his promise to represent the class as "the poster child for oral hygiene and corrective mouth apparati."

As Vlad was driven away from school, he rolled down his window and waved a handkerchief at his friends.

"I won't let you down!" he yelled. "Thank you for believing in me!"

After twenty minutes of grinding, whirring, gluing, pinching, and poking, Dr. Greyson leaned back and said, "All done!" She handed Vlad a mirror.

Vlad smiled his fangiest smile at his reflection.* His teeth looked . . . just like before.

"Where . . . are my braces?"

"They're right there. They're infused with invisibility serum, so you don't have to worry about them changing your look."

Vlad ran his tongue across his teeth. Sure enough, he felt two rows of brackets and a thin wire across his uppers and lowers. "But . . . can you make them visible?"

"How would I possibly do that?" asked Dr. Greyson. "With some sort of *visibility* ray? That's impossible. Oh, what a silly thought."

---

* YOU MIGHT HAVE BEEN TOLD THAT VAMPIRES DO NOT HAVE REFLECTIONS. THIS WAS TRUE IN THE OLD DAYS BECAUSE MIRRORS WERE ORIGINALLY MADE OF GLASS ATOP SILVER. IN MODERN TIMES, MIRRORS ARE MADE WITH ALUMINUM, WHICH HAS NO EFFECT ON VAMPIRES.

Dr. Greyson removed Vlad's bib and let him choose a toy from a box. Vlad absent-mindedly picked a plush Snail Pal and slunk out of the room in defeat. As he passed through the lobby, he saw Lobo flipping through a magazine.

"Hey, Lobo," said Vlad. "What's up?"

"I'm finally getting my braces off!" Lobo beamed. "A whoole year without corn

on the cob. I'm gonna be like *NOM NOM NOM!*"

Vlad tugged at his Snail Pal's eyeball. "Sounds great."

"And what are you going to be excited to have when you finally get yours off?" asked Lobo.

Vlad let out a thirty-second sigh. "Perfect teeth, I guess."

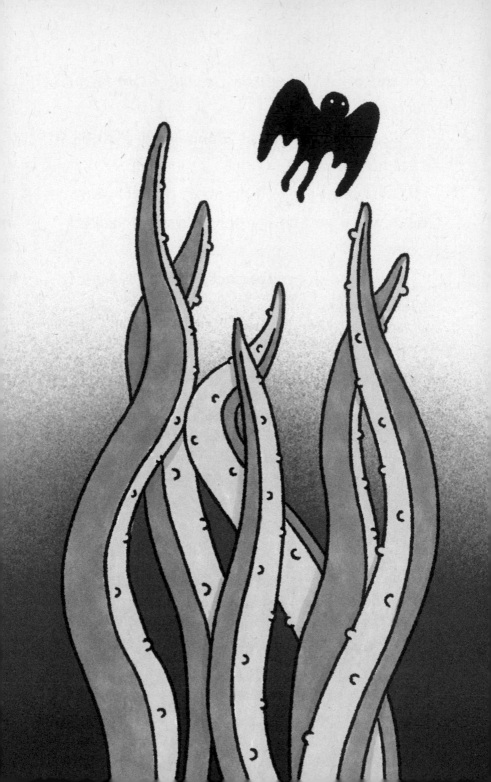

ŒΔå◊𝖽 ô•𝖘Ü

𝖙Ü≥Ü ≥Ü•ʃ 𝖽Ü" Ωå≤◊≥¥¥œ≤ ꜱꜱΣ •𝖘ə≈𝖘¥Üô ÜåÜœ℧Σ𝖘◊℧, ꜱꜱ͠≈əꜱ ¥Σå℧ ¥ΣôΔℲ 𝖘℧Ω𝖙Ü≥/√•ꜱΣΩꜱꜱ√å/ Ωə≤𝖘•μꜱꜱΣ/åəℲΩ𝖙 œ¥Σꜱꜱ𝖘¥≤. Œ≤. . . . Ü•ΣÜ ꜱ͠ œ¥≥Ü 𝖘𝖙Σ Ω√≈å℧ ¥𝖽 𝖙Σμåꜱꜱ• ꜱꜱ𝖘 åå. Œ≤. . . . Ü•ΣÜ . . . •¥≥𝖘 ¥𝖽 ΩœÜ "ꜱ𝖘𝖙 𝖘𝖙Ü ꜱ•åΣμ. ≤¥œÜ ≤Ü •𝖙Ü ΩœÜ "ꜱ𝖘𝖙 𝖘𝖙Ü •åΣÜ𝖘. Λ𝖘 ΣÜ •𝖘Ü, 𝖘𝖙Ü /ꜱꜱμ≤ å¥ . . . Ü 𝖙Ü≤.

Λ𝖘 ℧Ω𝖑𝖙œ, Œ•μ . . . . Ü•ΣÜ🜚 ≤å√•Üμ 𝖘℧𝖘Ωå℧ •Σ 𝖙Ü≤ μ℧•ʃ. "Δ´ʃˆ¥°Δ•˜μʃ𝖙𝖘ø."

187

"Arcane Yam Stew" 9:40 75°

≈Ʊ ϝϝƱ ∂åƱꙅꙅΣ© ΩϝꝴꙄꙄΙ ¥∂ ©¥¥, "ϝꙅꙅΩϝ
ϝμ ≈ƱƱΣ ¥ . . . Ʊ≳å¥¥ꙄƱμ "ϝƱΣ . . . åμ
Σμ ≈¥≈≈Ʊ ≳Ʊꝴ≳ϝƱμ. ≈¥≈≈Ʊ ≳Ʊ∂ååꝴ≳∂Ʊμ
ϝꙅꙅ≳ œꙅꙅ≳≳ꙅꙅΣ© ©å¥≈. Œ≳. . . . Ʊ≳ΣƱ
μ≳¥√√Ʊμ . . . åμ ≈ΩΙ ꙅΣ ϝꙅꙅ≳ ≳Ʊϝ.

189

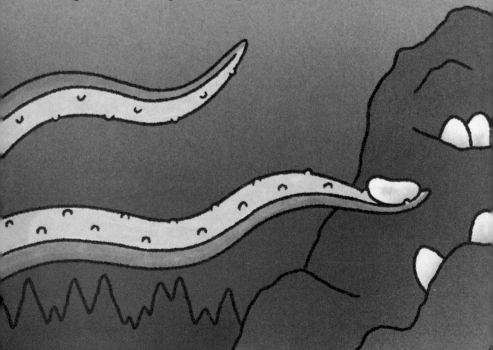

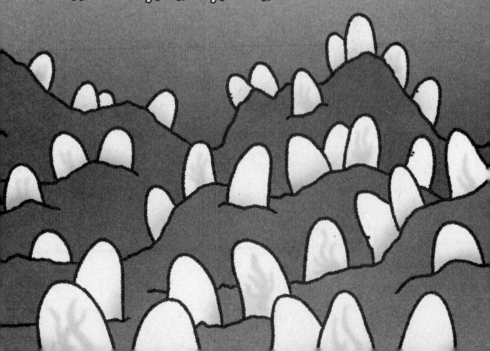

"√˜μς˜ς≈ςðœΣ´®." ⌄⫩ſſμ Œ⌄. . . . Ʊ⫩ΣƱ.

ʌå̊å⫩⫩Ʊ œ¥ . . . Ʊμ ∮¥ Σ¥∮∮Ʊ⫩ Ʊœ√∮Ʊ μƱ⌄ſ.

¶ª©°Δ˙ð . . . Ë♪Δ●ς∮ i⌄μ⫩ ÿΩⱾ̊íị˜," ⌄⫩ſſμ Œ⌄. . . . Ʊ⫩ΣƱ.

"∮∮∮´⌄ ¥ʃƱ, Œ⌄. . . . Ʊ⫩ΣƱ," ⌄⫩ſſμ ©⫩ſſðð. "ſſ μſſμΣ´∮ ⌄ƱƱ œƱ ∮∮Ʊ⫩Ʊ, Ʊſſ∮∮Ʊ⫩."

Œ⌄. . . . Ʊ⫩ΣƱ "∮¥¥⌄∮Ʊμ ſſΣ Σμ ˜∮ΩʃƱμ ∮ƱΣ∮ΩåƱ ©ſſΣ⌄∮ ∮∮Ʊ ˚å̊å ∮¥ ©Ʊ∮ ∮∮Ʊ Ωå̊⌄⌄´⌄ ∮∮ƱΣ∮ſſ¥Σ: ¶Σ⌄°Δ˙ ð°Δ˙ðΣœi£⌄."

÷ðɛµ℧ ©¥ʂ ðɛ⋁ Ʃµ ʂðɛ≥Ʃ℧µ ¥ðð ʂ≺ʘ⨍℧
åʂʂ©⨍ʂ≤ ¥ℲℲΔðℿ ◊≠ÿ℧åµ¶ɳ µℲ∆ᴅÈ⊤Ɵᴗ
⨍ꟼǫºʂô̂θΔˇœ •ᴗℲ‡Ɵᴖ.

"ʃå°Δðʃª⁻ʂʂ," ≤ʂʂµ Œ≤. . . . ℧≥Ʃ℧. "ʓ∞å
º⌠≤µ~å°≠ ðɛℲ. ℧œʂʂ Ʃ´ʂʂ≤⌠Ó̈ï î´‰~ıꟼ!"

"Ωᴗ¥¥å," ≤ʂʂµ ðʂΣ⌠ʂʂ℧.

"Ɇœ, ℧℧⨍," ≤ʂʂµ ℧≥ʂʂʃ. "Ω¥¥å."

"ÅÜʂ´≤ λℲℲᴗ ‡ô̂ð• ⊦ΛꞴ©℧ʂ Ɵᴖʘʂɳʂ⨍ʂʂ
≤‡ʂʂ≈ʂʂµ℧⁻≤‡¥¥ ¥Σ ʂ‡℧."

ELISE SHIPS OUT

After a few short weeks in Creep's Cove, it was time for Elise and her mom to return to the mainland. Jagged Rocks Resort, Spa, and Portal to the Underworld was closed until the next equinox, and all the seasonal witches had flown, sailed, or teleported back to their homes around the world.

Elise had an uncomfortable feeling. She had just gotten used to being around these obnoxious, chaotic kids, and suddenly she

195

was standing in front of them saying good-
bye.

"When will you be back?" asked Quade.

"I might be back in six months for a little
bit. Maybe over the summer for a while."

"Begin.Transmission...," beeped Allie. "This.
Being.Is.Experiencing.Mild.Discomfort . . .
End.Transmission."

"This is the *actual* worst day of my *miserable* life!" wailed Lizzie. "I feel like I'm going to have to take out my sadness on others."

"Great," said Vlad. "Are you sure you can't stay, Elise?"

"Yeah," said Elise.

She scanned the class. Some heads were hanging low. Some kids were trying to smile and be strong for her, one was actively sobbing, and one was crying silently and invisibly.

The last time Elise had felt this particular uncomfortable feeling, she'd turned a few kids into slugs. It had helped a little. *So,* she thought, *who should I bring with me? Lobo seems like a good option. Low maintenance, loyal. Quade is really nice. He'd probably make a sweet slug. Who else . . . Gilly? She's*

already kinda slimy, so it wouldn't be that big of an adjustment. Or maybe Erik. He would—

"We got you something," said Frankie. Frankie carried a box to Elise. Elise took the lid off, and inside were a couple of toys, a book, and a stack of stamped envelopes.

"These are all addressed to the school," said Elise.

"Aye," said Gilly. "For ye to write to us."

"I calculated the postage," said Frankie. "The mermaid postal system is *fascinating.* Anyway, look underneath."

Elise lifted the stack of envelopes and found a bunch of folded sheets of paper in assorted shapes, sizes, colors, and smells.

"WE WRIIIIITE LETTERS, TOO," groaned Emma.

"To read on the long voyage back," added Erik.

"I wrote my letter on some deli slices," glirped Bobby. "In case you get hungry."

"Yeah, and we'll keep it going until you come back," said Vlad. "I call it being 'pen pals.' Good, right?"

"Nice one, Vlad," said Griff, stifling his tears.

"I CAN'T DO IT!" screamed Lizzie. Lizzie ran straight for Elise with her ridiculous little forelegs out. Elise braced herself for a tackling hug, but instead Lizzie grabbed an

action figure from Elise's box. "I tried. I *tried* to send Dino Rusty with you, bestie, but I can't. I just can't!" Lizzie clutched Dino Rusty to her chest and returned to the group.

Elise thought back to her trip across the

sea to Creep's Cove. She clutched her box of letters and gazed at her new friends. She decided against turning any of them into slugs.

She wasn't alone anymore. Her coven was always with her.

However, you might be surprised to know that sometimes I get a little... stressed out.

See, there are only three things that annoy me:

1. The slightest inconvenience.

2. Not getting exactly what I want.

3. Surprises.

When I'm reading a book, I don't like twists and turns.

I want to go in knowing what to expect.

And I want the same for you.

So here's what's going
to happen in the next
TERRIBLES book.

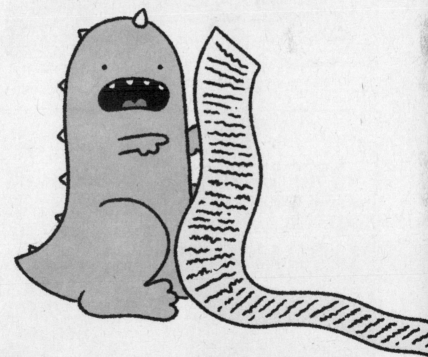

Story by spoiled story.

We get challenged to a game of creepoball by some gnomes.

And we learn about them.

pointy hats

falling object protec- tion

usually red or green

There's also a weird goose.

Griff, Emma, and Bobby
decide they like being "extreme."

air quotes

But they take things
waaaaay too far.

Like...
dimensionally
too far.

Oh! There are some letters to and from my bestie, Elise.

Vlad, Erik, and Allie get their "band" back together.

Vlad's outfit is ridiculous.

Their music is okay.

And we learn about everyone's hobbies.

ALLIE'S HOBBY IS DISGUSTING.

My poem is the best.

Poems are easy to write, by the way.

Lobo's grandmother is a ghost.

And she decides to
stop, like, being one.

We destroy the gnomes at creepoball.

I mean, we absolutely and fully cream their corn.

(leaving in shame)

Let's see. We all go to the Big Pile of Junk.

Nobody makes anything good.

Then I have the greatest day of my entire life.

The end.

213

BIO ALERT!

TRAVIS NICHOLS is the author and illustrator of a tidy heap of award-winning books and comics for kids and post-kids. When he's not writing and drawing, he's collecting and/or abandoning hobbies and representing Earth as an Adjunct Consulate in the Intergalactic Consortium. He lives in Brooklyn, New York, with some of his favorite creatures. You can find him puttering around in the garden.

IAMTRAVISNICHOLS.COM

🐦 @TRAVISNICHOLS

📷 @IAMTRAVISNICHOLS